This book is dedicated to:
the humane societies and rescue
organizations that care for animals in need,
Bob Goebel, who flew jets during his
Air Force career, and
to my rescue dog, Bonita.

Bonita Finds a Forever Home: A True Story

Story © 2015 by Suzanne M. Malpass, suzanne@straddlebooks.com
Illustrations © 2015 by Trish Morgan, trish@peachbloomhill.com

PRT0615A

Printed in the United States
Library of Congress Control Number: 2015907050
ISBN-13: 978-1-63177-275-7

www.mascotbooks.com

BONITA
Finds a Forever Home
A True Story

Suzanne M. Malpass

Illustrated by Trish Morgan

Best Wishes,
Suzanne M. Malpass

At her birth home, a tiny poodle-mix had no name. She was much smaller than her two brothers. The three tumbled over each other to get milk from their mother.

When the puppies were six weeks old,
families came to see them. The five-year-old
Stone twins saw the littlest. Anna picked her up.
"Can we get this one, Mama?" Lucas asked.
"Pleeeeeease?" Anna begged.

All the way home, the twins talked about names for their new buddy. When they saw their friend Dave's big brother, both blurted out, "Bo!"

A few days later, the children ran into the kitchen. "Something's wrong with Bo!" Anna yelled. "Hurry, Mama, hurry!" Lucas cried.

All three rushed into the living room
and stared at Bo. Her whole body shook. She
breathed way too fast and way too hard.

"I think she's scared," said Major Stone as
she picked Bo up. Even held tightly, the little
puppy could not stop shaking.

In time, the family got to know Bo. At
dinner one night Lucas said, "Bo can race
even faster than I can."
"And she jumps really high when she's
excited," Anna added.

Sadly, her people also figured out when Bo panicked. It was every time a jet warmed up, took off or landed. That happened very often on the huge Air Force base.

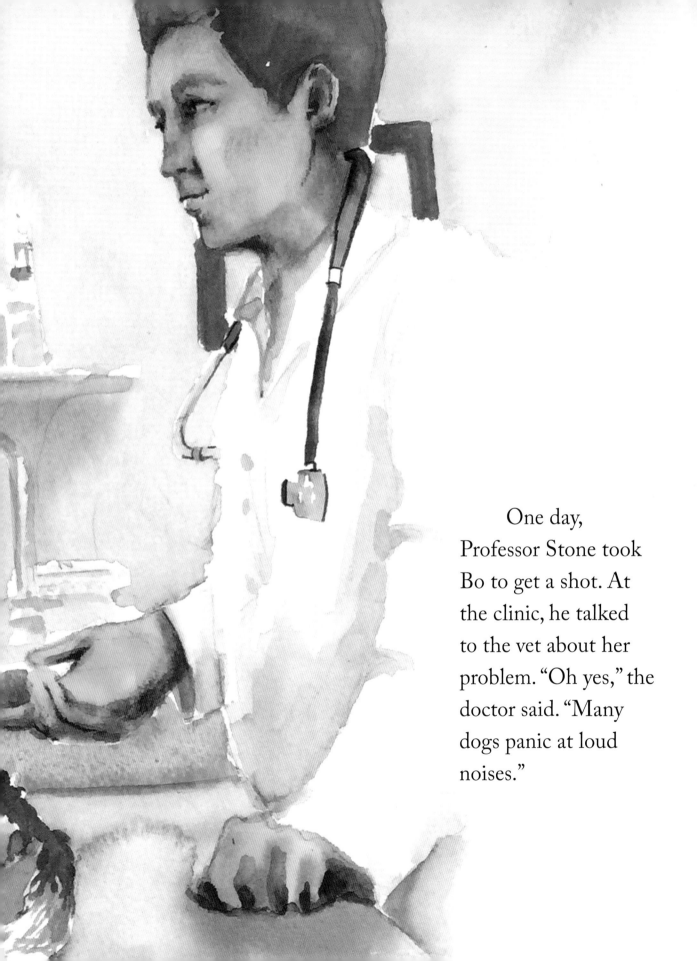

One day, Professor Stone took Bo to get a shot. At the clinic, he talked to the vet about her problem. "Oh yes," the doctor said. "Many dogs panic at loud noises."

In the end, the family had to take Bo to the animal shelter. The roar of the jets was just too much for her. In tears Anna asked, "Can you find a quiet home for Bo?"

The lady behind the desk smiled. "I'm sure we can."

"We still want her," Lucas sniffed. "But the jets scare her silly."

The people at the shelter got Bo ready for a new home. A vet cleaned her teeth and spayed her. A worker put her picture up on the web.

Not far away a woman was still crying over losing her dog, Hunter. When she saw Bo's photo on the web, Suzanne grabbed her cell phone and dialed. "Could I come and see that little poodle-mix tomorrow?" she asked.

Suzanne visited Bo, fell in love and brought her home. On the phone, she told her husband Jeff about their new friend. "Bo is a boy's name," she said. "So I call her Bonita. What do you think?"

The husband didn't really want a new dog. Still he said, "Okay, I guess." But when he met Bonita, he fell for her, too.

Three days later, Jeff was as worried as his wife. Their little dog lay very still inside the animal hospital. She looked more dead than alive. The vet said, "It's a good thing you brought her in. Both lungs show signs of fluid."

"Will she be okay?" Jeff asked.

"We've only had her for a week, but we already love her," Suzanne added.

After two long days, the couple was finally able to see Bonita again. "Wow! She looks sooooo much better!" said Suzanne.

"I think she'll be fine now," the doctor said. "Give her one pill a day until they're gone."

Bonita is an only dog in her forever home. She loves to lick any skin she can reach. When she sees her leash, she races around and jumps up and down.

If you ever want a friend like Bonita, visit your local shelter. There you can find a dog or a cat that would love to join your family.

About the Author:

Suzanne M. Malpass writes under her maiden name in hopes that her many relatives will buy the books when they see their surname on them. Her lifelong love of animals, children and words led to her series of non-fiction children's books, which feature animal rescues with happy endings. *Bonita Finds a Forever Home* is the sixth book in the series.

Other books by Suzanne M. Malpass:

Stony's Tale: A True Tombstone Story

Rusty Tries Growing Up: A True Eastern Shore Story

A Lab's Tale

Colorado, the Flying Horse: A True Arizona Story

Where's Our Siamese?: A True Story

Many thanks to my careful readers,
Jean Rubin, Matthew Rogers, Mark Rogers,
Anne Houser, Jody Clark and Hollyann M. Brown.
Many thanks also to my young consultants,
Hannah Wilder, Deborah Wilder, Suzi Ward
and Abby Ward.